Mahalia Mouse Goes to College

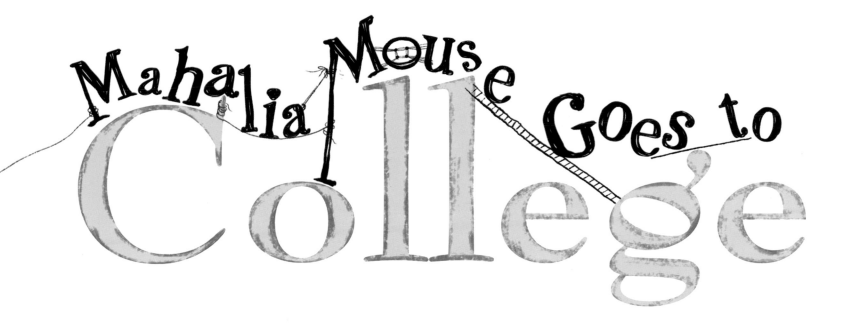

Mahalia Mouse Goes to College

John Lithgow
Illustrated by Igor Oleynikov

Simon & Schuster Books for Young Readers

New York   London   Toronto   Sydney

The skies of September were bursting with rain,
Pelting the old dormitory.
It filled every gutter and choked every drain.
Chapter 1 of Mahalia's story.

A family of mice huddled up to keep warm;
Their basement was flooded with water.
The mother peered out at the furious storm,
Then turned and addressed her young daughter.

"Mahalia, darling," she said with a sigh,
"Your father's not back till tomorrow.
So wrap up in newspaper, keep yourself dry,
And find us some cheese or a scrap of meat pie.
The children are starving. The babies may die!"
Then she faltered, consumed by her sorrow.

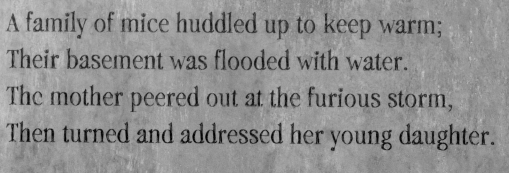

Mahalia hugged her, then scampered outside,
Sheltered by clumps of wisteria.
In minutes she'd found a secure place to hide,
In a hall by the dorm cafeteria.

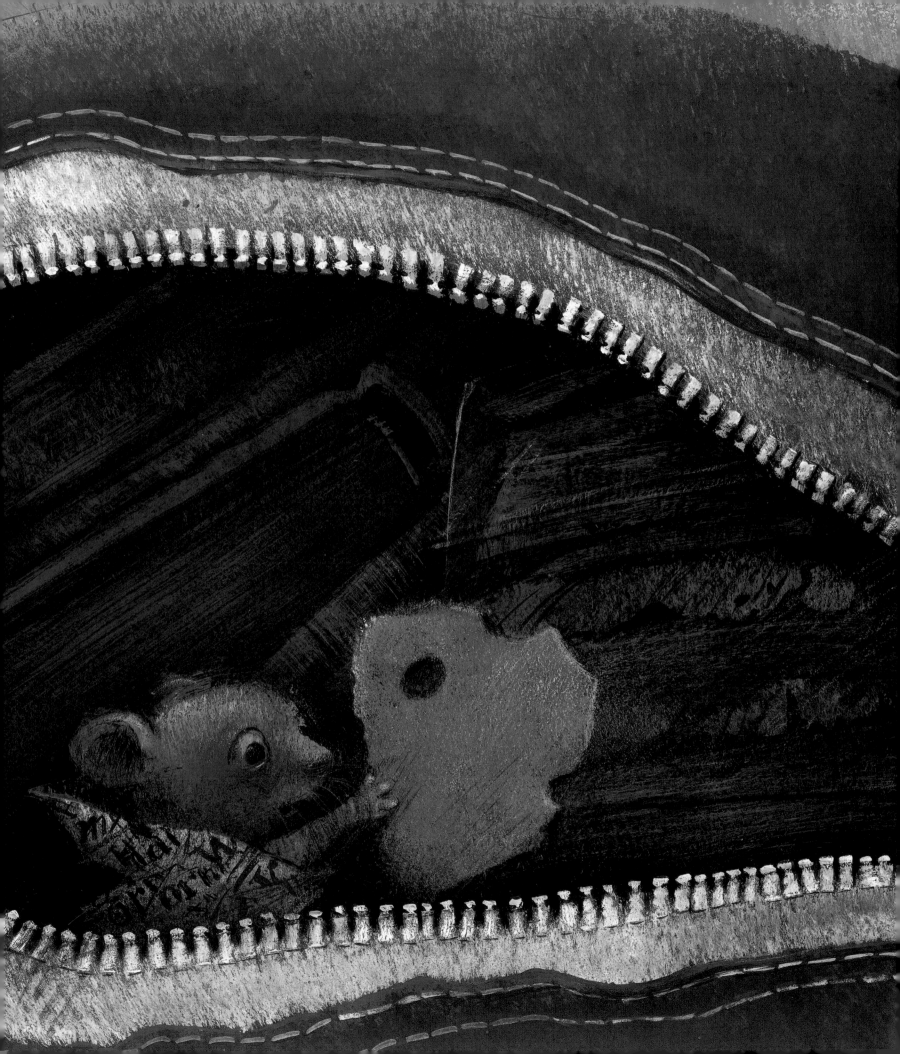

Nearby lay a backpack, unclaimed on the floor,
Smelling of cheese and roast beef.
Mahalia climbed up inside to explore,
Like a seasoned, self-confident thief.

She found a fat sandwich and plucked out the cheese,
Stuffing it into her sack.
But suddenly—*zip!*—a sharp sound made her freeze,
As everything faded to black.

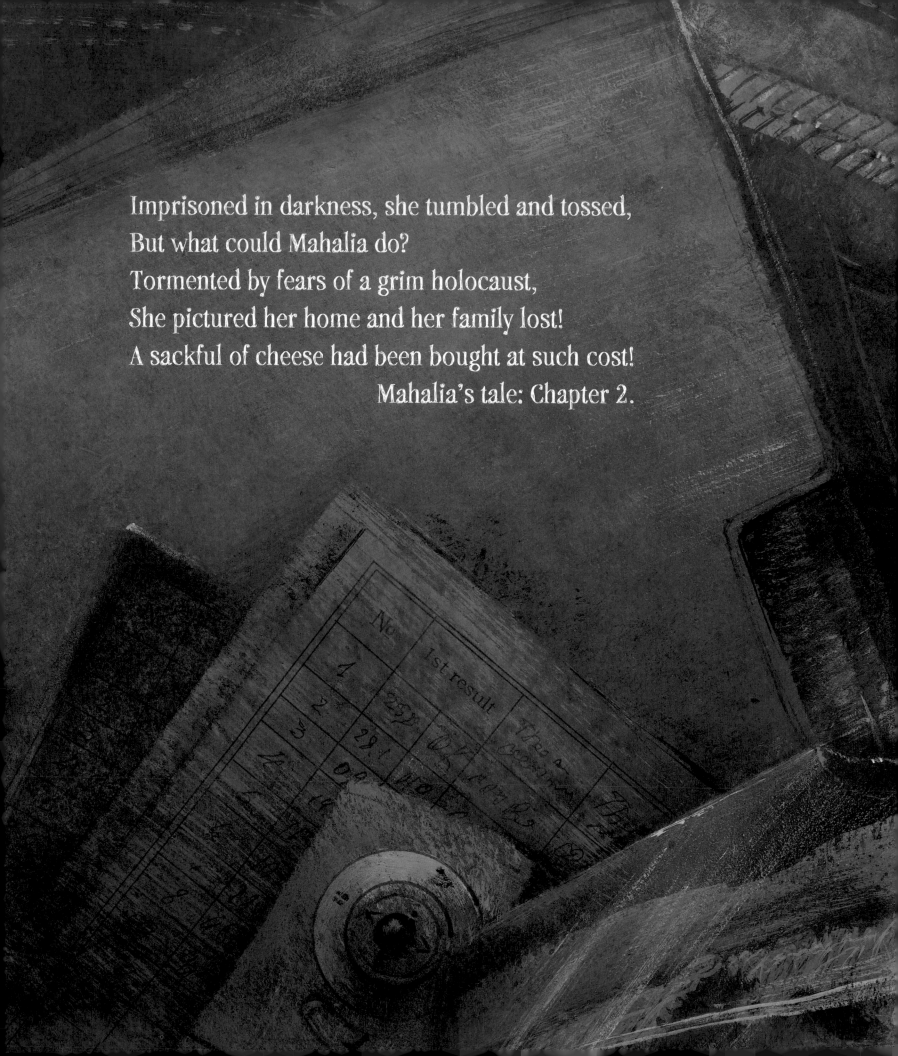

Imprisoned in darkness, she tumbled and tossed,
But what could Mahalia do?
Tormented by fears of a grim holocaust,
She pictured her home and her family lost!
A sackful of cheese had been bought at such cost!

Mahalia's tale: Chapter 2.

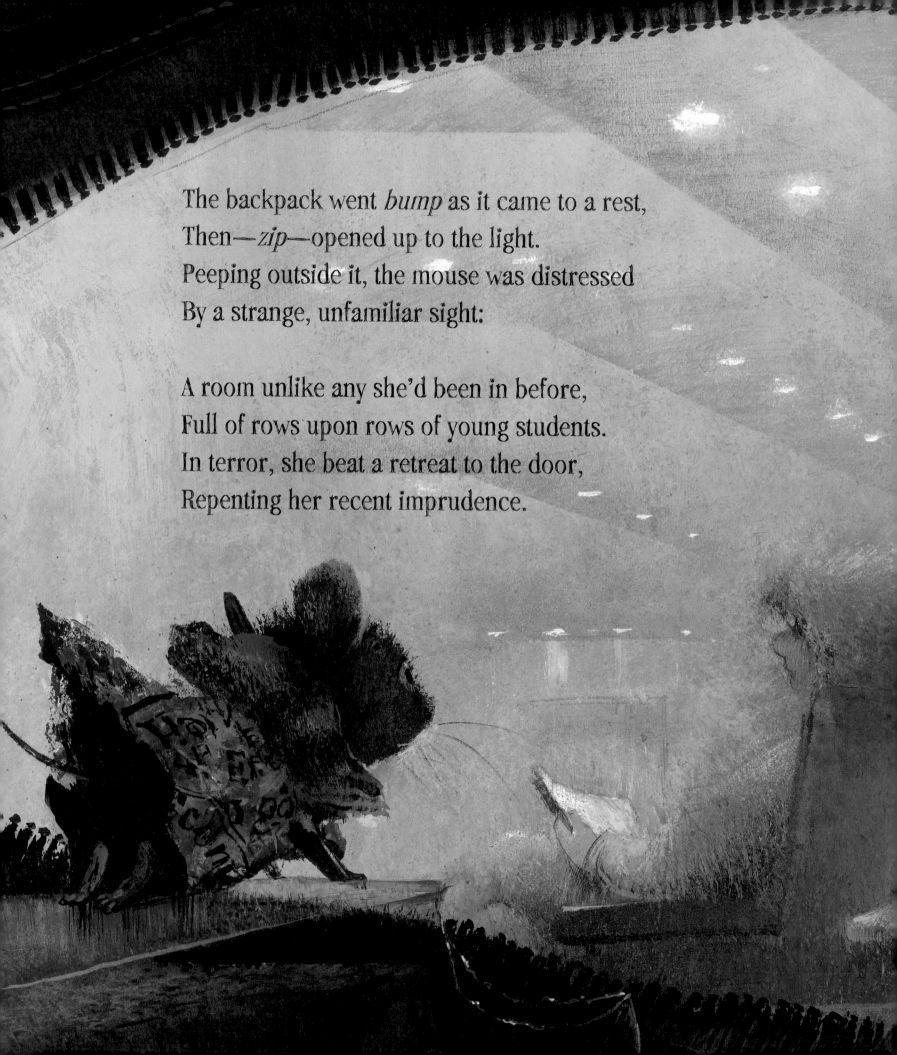

The backpack went *bump* as it came to a rest,
Then—*zip*—opened up to the light.
Peeping outside it, the mouse was distressed
By a strange, unfamiliar sight:

A room unlike any she'd been in before,
Full of rows upon rows of young students.
In terror, she beat a retreat to the door,
Repenting her recent imprudence.

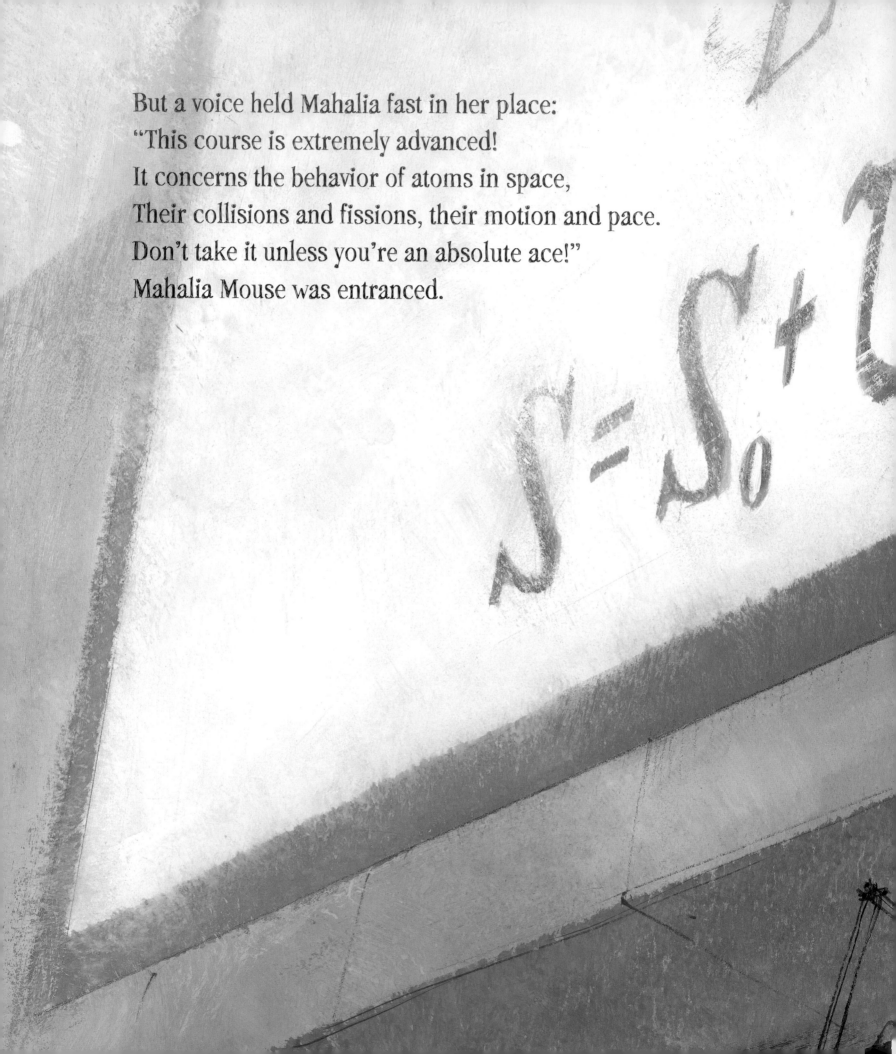

But a voice held Mahalia fast in her place:
"This course is extremely advanced!
It concerns the behavior of atoms in space,
Their collisions and fissions, their motion and pace.
Don't take it unless you're an absolute ace!"
Mahalia Mouse was entranced.

In her lonely new lodgings, she took the course on,
Overwhelmed by its daunting regime.
But one night as she slept, in the hour before dawn,
Her mother appeared in a dream.

"My baby," she said in a quavering voice,
"You're off to a wonderful start.
Don't think about us; just believe in your choice.
Be happy and follow your heart!"

Thereafter, whenever she sneaked into class,
The mouse would recall every word.
But one day, in the midst of a lecture, alas!
The unthinkable finally occurred!

"A MOUSE!!"

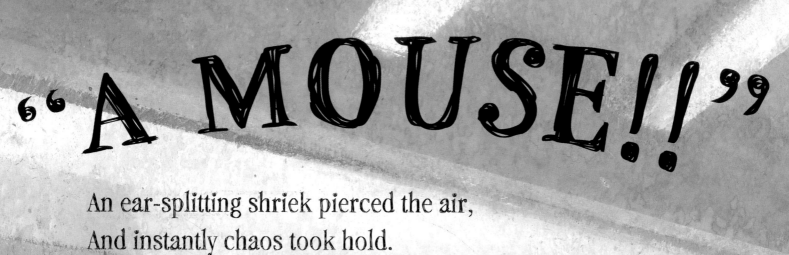

An ear-splitting shriek pierced the air,
And instantly chaos took hold.
"WHERE?" people screamed. "OVER THERE! OVER THERE!"
Some ran for an exit, some leaped on a chair.
Mahalia, trembling with fright and despair,
Felt the blood in her body run cold.

The professor stepped forward to calm the class down.

He stood at Mahalia's side.

He stared at her notes with a studious frown.

"This mouse is a genius!" he cried.

"Her grasp of the subject is sharp as a blade!

This rodent will study with ME!"

By noon he had kept the bold promise he'd made:

Her books were all purchased, her lab fees were paid.

Her doubts and her fears were completely allayed.

Mahalia Mouse: Chapter 3.

That day marked the start of four glorious years:
Mahalia Mouse went to college.
Admired and respected by all of her peers,
She gathered a broad range of knowledge.

Along with her major, she dabbled in art,
In history, math, and zoology.
But one course especially captured her heart:
The Basics of Human Psychology.

Activities, too, filled Mahalia's days
(For no shrinking violet, she):
Fencing and football, recitals and plays,
Glee club and squash, a brief square-dancing phase.
At the end of four years of achievement and praise,
It was time to receive her degree.

As she giddily braced for her June graduation,
A hundred reporters all sought her.
And that's how her parents, in wild jubilation,
Stumbled on news of their daughter.

At commencement Mahalia marched with her class,
Perched on a friend's brawny shoulder.
Thousands of well-wishers saw the mouse pass,
Craning their necks to behold her.

All at once she went pale. Her palms were like ice.
Her face wore a stricken expression.
Her eyes were transfixed by a family of mice
Crouched alongside the procession!

"MY MOTHER! MY FATHER!" Mahalia cried
As she skittered on down to the ground.
When she landed, her family rushed to her side,
Exploding with love, with relief, and with pride,
A jumble of feelings too joyous to hide,
For the child they had lost had been found.

And so we take leave of Mahalia's tale,
A story of stout self-reliance;
An epic account on a miniature scale
Of a mouse who set forth on life's bumpy trail
And succeeded by simply refusing to fail:
Mahalia, Bachelor of Science.

To the Harvard College class of 2005

—J. L.

To all children, little but persistent

—I. O.

Acknowledgments
The author acknowledges Jim Harrison and Professor Jeremy Knowles.

SIMON & SCHUSTER BOOKS FOR YOUNG READERS • An imprint of Simon & Schuster Children's Publishing Division • 1230 Avenue of the Americas, New York, New York 10020 • Text copyright © 2007 by John Lithgow • Illustrations copyright © 2007 by Art and Design Agency "PiArt" • All rights reserved, including the right of reproduction in whole or in part in any form. • SIMON & SCHUSTER BOOKS FOR YOUNG READERS is a trademark of Simon & Schuster, Inc. • Book design by Dan Potash • The text for this book is set in Stanyan. • The illustrations for this book are rendered in gouache, then digitally treated. • Manufactured in China

2 4 6 8 10 9 7 5 3 1

Library of Congress Cataloging-in-Publication Data • Lithgow, John, 1945– Mahalia Mouse goes to college / John Lithgow ; illustrated by Igor Oleynikov. — 1st ed. • p. cm. • Summary: Sent by her parents to find food, Mahalia Mouse finds herself trapped in a backpack and transported to a physics classroom at Harvard University, where she discovers an aptitude for science. • ISBN-13: 978-1-4169-2715-0 • ISBN-10: 1-4169-2715-8 • [1. Mice—Fiction. 2. Harvard University—Fiction. 3. Universities and colleges—Fiction. 4. Stories in rhyme.] I. Oleynikov, Igor, ill. • II. Title. • PZ8.3.L6375Tal 2007 • [E]—dc22 • 2005036238

John Lithgow's performance of *Mahalia Mouse Goes to College* was recorded April 11, 2005, and is an excerpt from his live commencement address to the Harvard University class of 2005.